THE TWELVE DAYS OF CHRISTMAS

Laurel Long

Dial Books

an imprint of Penguin Group (USA) Inc.

DIAL BOOKS
An imprint of Penguin Group (USA) Inc.
Published by The Penguin Group
Penguin Group (USA) Inc.
375 Hudson Street, New York, NY 10014, U.S.A.

Penguin Group (Canada), 90 Eglinton Avenue East, Suite 700, Toronto, Ontario,
Canada M4P 2Y3 (a division of Pearson Penguin Canada Inc.) • Penguin
Books Ltd, 80 Strand, London WC2R 0RL, England • Penguin Ireland, 25 St.
Stephen's Green, Dublin 2, Ireland (a division of Penguin Books Ltd) • Penguin
Group (Australia), 250 Camberwell Road, Camberwell, Victoria 3124, Australia
(a division of Pearson Australia Group Pty Ltd) • Penguin Books India Pvt Ltd,
11 Community Centre, Panchsheel Park, New Delhi - 110 017, India • Penguin
Group (NZ), 67 Apollo Drive, Rosedale, Auckland 0632, New Zealand (a division
of Pearson New Zealand Ltd) • Penguin Books (South Africa) (Pty) Ltd, 24
Sturdee Avenue, Rosebank, Johannesburg 2196, South Africa • Penguin Books
Ltd, Registered Offices: 80 Strand, London WC2R 0RL, England

The publisher does not have any control over and does not assume any
responsibility for author or third-party websites or their content.
Designed by Nancy R. Leo-Kelly
Text set in Cochin
Manufactured in China on acid-free paper
1 3 5 7 9 10 8 6 4 2

Library of Congress Cataloging-in-Publication Data

Long, Laurel.
The twelve days of Christmas / Laurel Long.
p.   cm.
Summary: An illustrated version of the traditional song.
ISBN 978-0-8037-3357-2
1. Folk songs, English—England—Texts. 2. Christmas music—Texts.
[1. Folk songs—England. 2. Christmas music.] I. Title.
PZ8.3.L85Tw 2009 782.42—dc22 2008015774

The art for this book was created using oil paints.

Sheet music provided by Musicnotes.com. Copyright 2009 Musicnotes, Inc.
All rights reserved.
Music composition by Bob Sherwin.

For Sara

On the first day of Christmas,
My true love gave to me
A partridge in a pear tree.

On the second day of Christmas,
My true love gave to me
Two turtle doves,
And a partridge in a pear tree.

3

On the third day of Christmas,
My true love gave to me
Three French hens,
Two turtle doves,
And a partridge in a pear tree.

4

On the fourth day of Christmas,
My true love gave to me
Four collie birds,
Three French hens,
Two turtle doves,
And a partridge in a pear tree.

5

On the fifth day of Christmas,
My true love gave to me
Five golden rings,
Four collie birds,
Three French hens,
Two turtle doves,
And a partridge in a pear tree.

On the sixth day of Christmas,
My true love gave to me
Six geese a-laying,
Five golden rings,
Four collie birds,
Three French hens,
Two turtle doves,
And a partridge in a pear tree.

7

On the seventh day of Christmas,
My true love gave to me
Seven swans a-swimming,
Six geese a-laying,
Five golden rings,
Four collie birds,
Three French hens,
Two turtle doves,
And a partridge in a pear tree.

On the eighth day of Christmas,
My true love gave to me
Eight maids a-milking,
Seven swans a-swimming,
Six geese a-laying,
Five golden rings,
Four collie birds,
Three French hens,
Two turtle doves,
And a partridge in a pear tree.

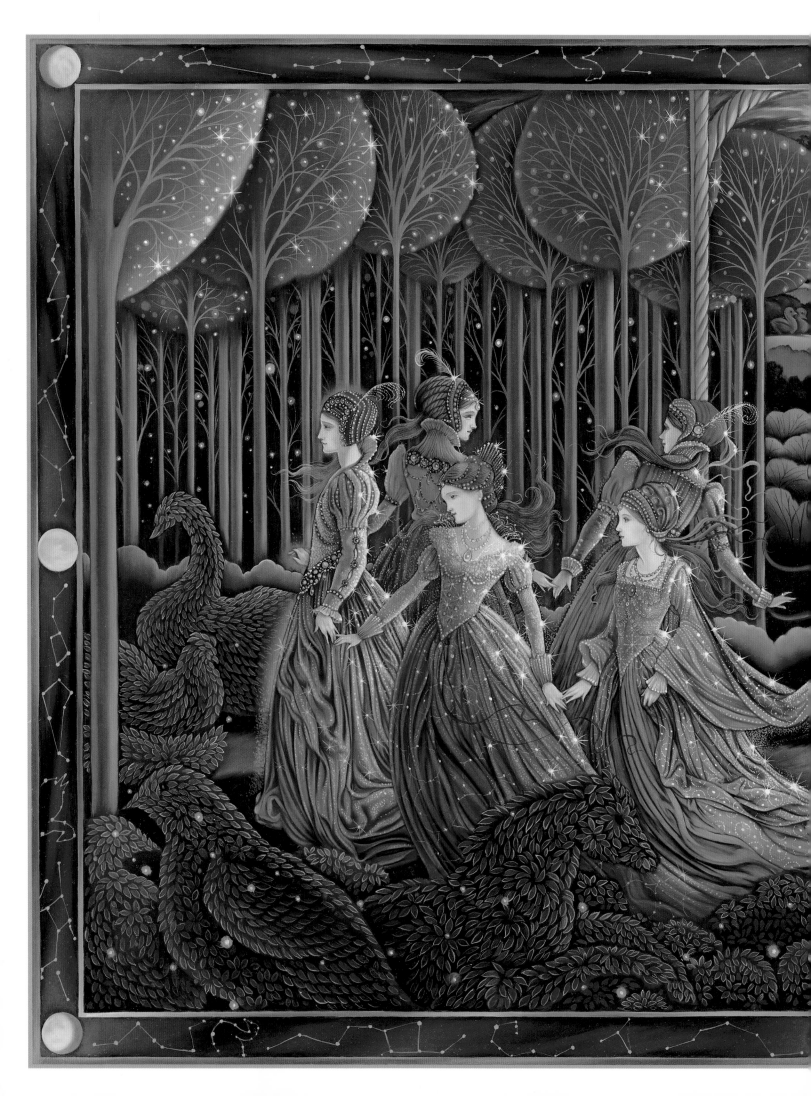

On the ninth day of Christmas,
My true love gave to me
Nine ladies dancing,
Eight maids a-milking,
Seven swans a-swimming,
Six geese a-laying,
Five golden rings,
Four collie birds,
Three French hens,
Two turtle doves,
And a partridge in a pear tree.

10

On the tenth day of Christmas,
My true love gave to me
Ten lords a-leaping,
Nine ladies dancing,
Eight maids a-milking,
Seven swans a-swimming,
Six geese a-laying,
Five golden rings,
Four collie birds,
Three French hens,
Two turtle doves,
And a partridge in a pear tree.

On the eleventh day of Christmas,
My true love gave to me
Eleven pipers piping,
Ten lords a-leaping,
Nine ladies dancing,
Eight maids a-milking,
Seven swans a-swimming,
Six geese a-laying,
Five golden rings,
Four collie birds,
Three French hens,
Two turtle doves,
And a partridge in a pear tree.

On the twelfth day of Christmas,
My true love gave to me
Twelve drummers drumming,
Eleven pipers piping,
Ten lords a-leaping,
Nine ladies dancing,
Eight maids a-milking,
Seven swans a-swimming,
Six geese a-laying,
Five golden rings,
Four collie birds,
Three French hens,
Two turtle doves,
And a partridge in a pear tree!

The Twelve Days

Moderately ♩ = 112

On the first day of Christ-mas my true love gave to me a par - tridge in a pear tree. On the

sec-ond day of Christ-mas my true love gave to me two tur - tle doves and a par - tridge in a pear

tree. On the third day of Christ-mas my true love gave to me three French hens, two tur - tle doves, and a

par - tridge in a pear tree. On the fourth day of Christ-mas my true love gave to me

four col - lie birds, three French hens, two tur - tle doves, and a par - tridge in a pear tree. On the

OF CHRISTMAS English Traditional Carol

fifth day of Christ-mas my true love gave to me five gold-en rings!

a tempo

four __ col-lie birds, three French hens, two __ tur-tle doves, and a par-tridge in a pear

Repeat through no. 12, adding one line each repetition.

tree. On the sixth day of Christ-mas my true love gave to me
seventh day etc...

6. six geese a-lay-ing,
7. sev-en swans a-swim-ming,
8. eight maids a-milk-ing,
9. nine la-dies danc-ing,
10. ten lords a-leap-ing,
11. 'lev pip-ers pip-ing,
12. twelve drum-mers drum-ming,

five gold-en rings! four __ col-lie birds, three French hens,

Through 11th day repeat. | Final ending after 12th day.

two __ tur-tle doves, and a par-tridge __ in a pear tree. On the tree.

Artist's Note

The Twelve Days of Christmas has mysterious origins and hidden meanings.

One thing is certain: The days are the twelve festive days that begin on Christmas Day, when Jesus was born and end on the Epiphany, when the three Magi visited him, culminating in the Twelfth Night feast.

"The Twelve Days of Christmas" was first published as a children's book called *Mirth Without Mischief* in England in 1780. However, there are three older versions. It is thought to have originated in France as a possible Twelfth Night memory game. The players would repeat previous verses and add one more. If a player made an error, he or she would have to give a kiss or a gift to someone else.

The phrase "a partridge in a pear tree" gives some evidence of the song's transition from its French origins. The pear tree is actually a *perdrix*, French for partridge and pronounced *per-dree*. The word was copied down incorrectly when the oral version of the game was transcribed from French to English. The original line would have been: *A partridge, une perdrix*.

There are many interpretations of the song's lyrics. One suggestion is that "The Twelve Days of Christmas" was a Christian song with secret references to the teachings of the faith, perhaps dating from the sixteenth-century religious wars in England. For example, some say that the lords a-leaping symbolized the Ten Commandments. However, the British believe that the ten lords a-leaping were Moorish dancers who performed during the Christmas feast.

The questions surrounding the history and symbolism of "The Twelve Days of Christmas" open it up to a variety of artistic approaches. My interpretation of "The Twelve Days of Christmas" is a visual story with as many hidden images as there are meanings. It is a story that describes a journey through time and place. The twelve days reminded me of the twelve months and the twelve hours on a clock. The repetition of the lyrics seems related to the repeating cycles of the seasons, the turns of the hands on a clock, the phases of the moon around the sun, and the dawn and dusk of each day. This version of "The Twelve Days of Christmas" is about the order and mystery of life, about nature with all of its certainties and surprises.